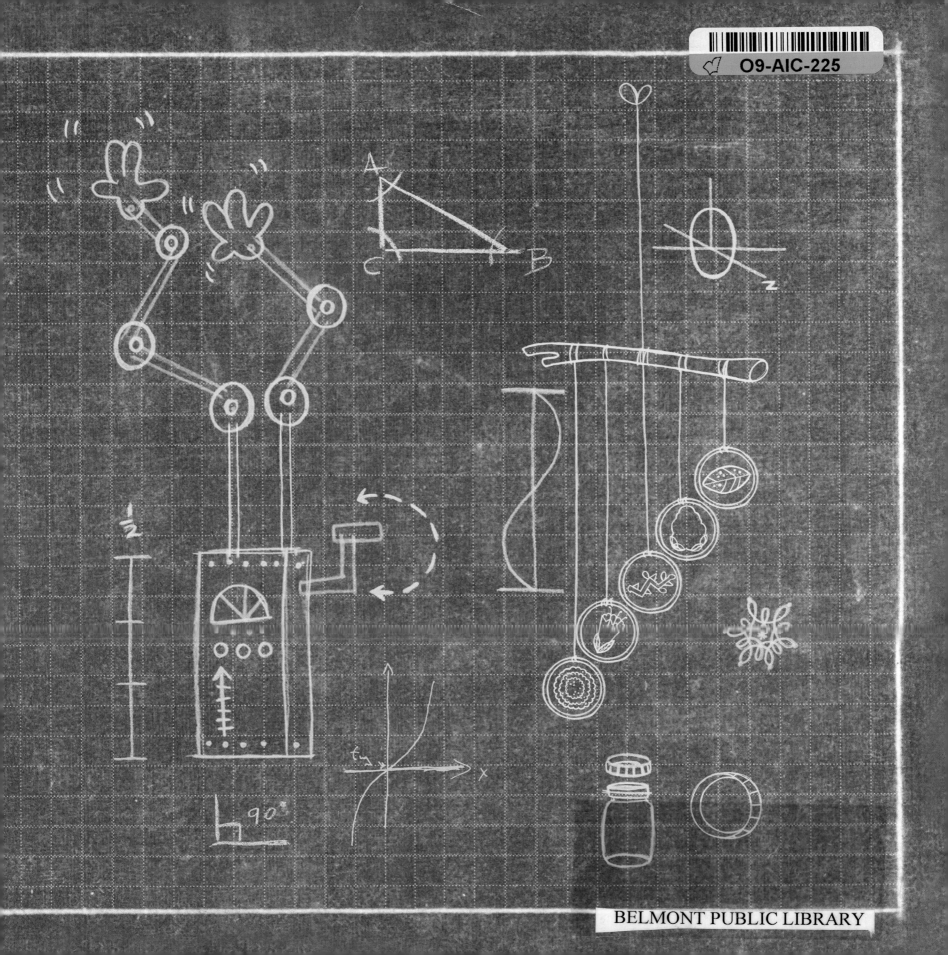

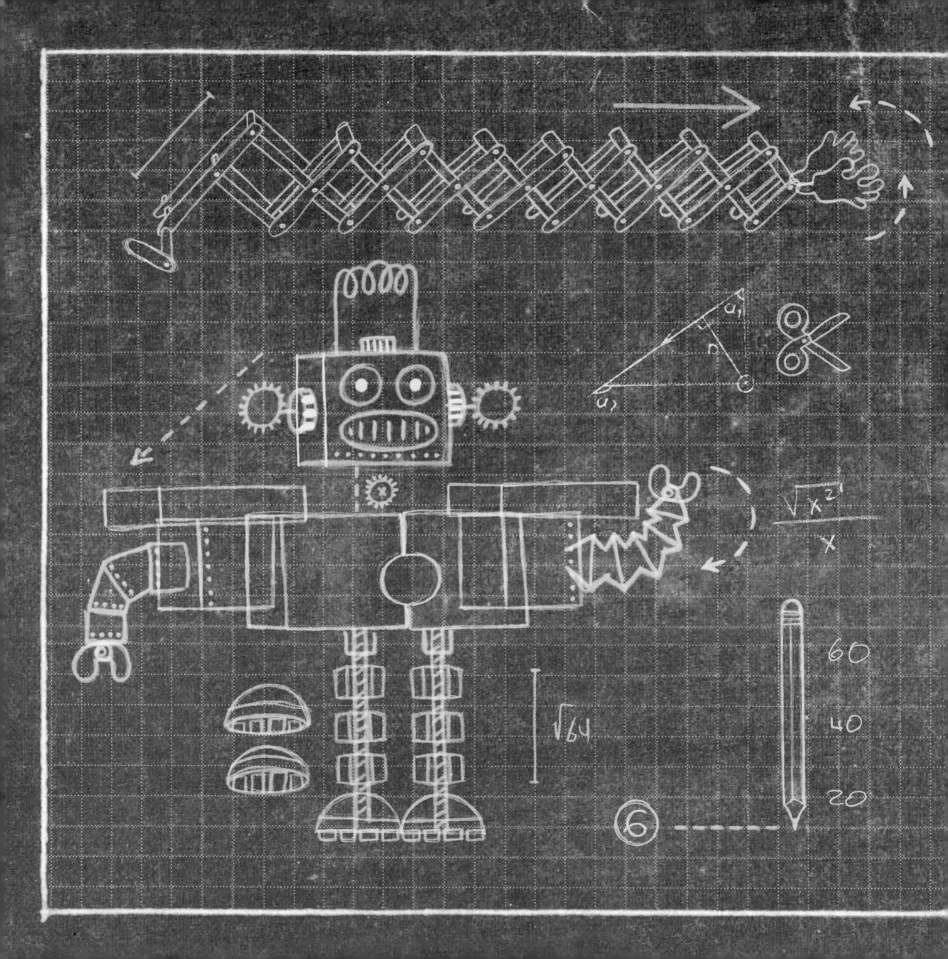

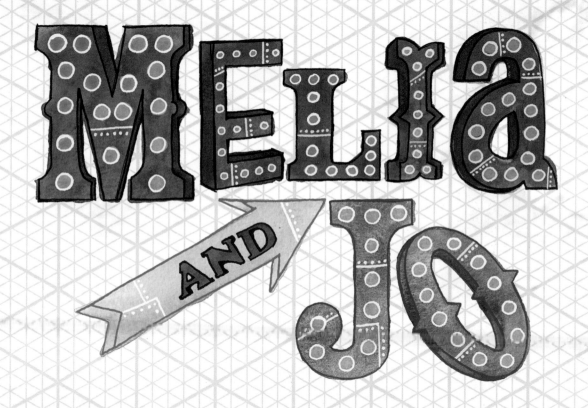

For Fox, Tallula, Jake, Anna,
and young creators everywhere!

Copyright © 2018 by Billy Aronson
Illustrations copyright © 2018 by Jennifer Oxley

hmhco.com

Library of Congress Cataloging-in-Publication Data is on file.
ISBN: 978-1-328-91626-6

Manufactured in China
SCP 10 9 8 7 6 5 4 3 2 1
4500709490

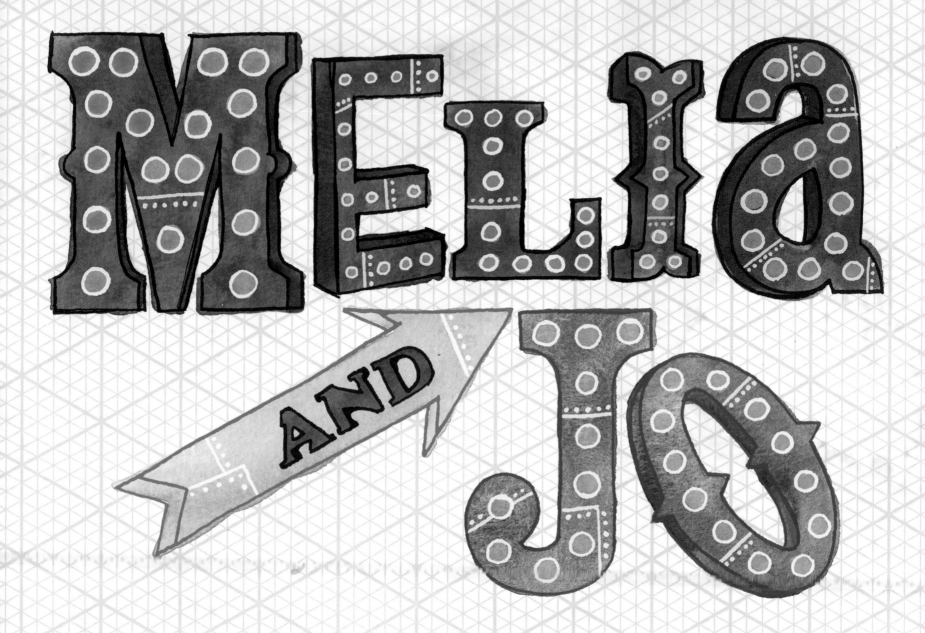

AMELIA AND JO

BILLY ARONSON & JENNIFER OXLEY

HOUGHTON MIFFLIN HARCOURT

Boston   New York

Melia loved science. Every day, in her backyard lab, she would create things that could scrub, pitch, tickle, bounce, fly, ding, or even make your bed.

3

Most of Melia's creations weren't finished. She just kept working on them. Measuring. Testing. Reading. Observing. Having a snack. Testing again.

And if the invention didn't work yet, she went through all those steps again!

One day, Melia was working on an airplane made of paper. She adjusted the wings. She adjusted the tail. She pulled the propeller a teeny bit further out. But still the plane wouldn't soar. How could she make it fly fast and far?

Suddenly, Melia heard a
strange sound! Growling?
Howling? Yelping?

The sound was coming from the girl
who had just moved in next door.

She seemed to be singing . . .

. . . while crouching and leaping around!

The girl came whirling and twirling toward Melia. "I'm Jo!" she said. "But you can call me JoJo. Or Josephine. Or Jo Jo Jo on the Go Go Go."

"I'm Melia," Melia replied. "You can call me Melia."

Melia started to explain that she was busy working on a really important invention, when Jo leaped right into Melia's lab.

"You've got so much cool stuff here, Melia Bo Belia!" said Jo as she flipped a bowl with an antenna and put it on her head.

"That's not a hat, actually," said Melia, carefully flipping it again.

Jo held up a bendy contraption and turned its crank. "I love this bendy ladder!"

"It's actually not a ladder," said Melia.

"Cool plane!" said Jo, picking up the paper plane and tossing it.

"CAREFUL!" said Melia.

As the plane plunged towards the mud, Melia dove to catch it.

Jo plucked a dandelion. "Too bad your plane doesn't fly like the fluff on a dandelion!" she said. *Puff!* The seeds went soaring in all directions.

Jo stopped to take a bite out of a licorice stick. Then she squealed, "*Oo, oo, oo, oo!* Check out the clubhouse balloon thing!" Jo poked her licorice stick into the neck of a small headless robot for safe keeping as she dashed toward the clubhouse.

That robot was one of Melia's favorite inventions! Its head kept falling off, but she loved it just the same.

"YOU CAN'T PUT A LICORICE STICK IN MY ROBOT!" Melia shouted.

Jo didn't even seem to hear. She skipped right back to her yard and started a new dance.

As Melia put her inventions back in order, she laughed about Jo's silly ideas. "She thought my cereal bowl radio was a hat!" But as Melia held the bowl upside down she began to wonder . . .

When Melia put her plane back, she remembered how Jo blew on the dandelion. Could Melia blow on the plane to make it soar?

Next, Melia reached for her headless robot—and gasped!

"With that sticky licorice in the robot's neck, the head stays right in place!" Melia was shocked. "Jo is a genius!"

Melia hurried over to Jo's yard. "Yo, Jo!" she called. But Jo didn't answer. She was creating a dance inspired by a leaping frog.

Melia came closer. "Can we be a team, Jo? Please, please, please?"

"No deal-ya, Melia," Jo replied, leaping higher and higher. "Why should I try to make a plane that soars when I can soar myself?"

"Watch out!" shouted Melia. But it was too late. Jo
had leapt so high, she'd gotten stuck on a tree branch.

"Hang on, Jo!" Melia dashed away and dashed right back with her crank contraption. As she turned the crank, its bendy ladder reached all the way up to the branch.

Jo scampered down the ladder. "Your inventions are the real deal, Meal!"

"I wouldn't have known this invention's true use if it weren't for you," said Melia. "It never worked as a spaghetti server. But when you called it a ladder, I realized it would be perfect for getting people down from trees!"

Melia brought out one invention after another to show Jo how she'd helped improve them. The antenna hat was perfect for listening to the radio while walking.

The licorice stick kept the robot's head on.

When she blew into the straw on the back of the plane, the plane could soar fast and far!

Jo realized that Melia was right: these two were meant to be together. They headed over to Melia's lab. "Sorry I yelled at you," said Melia. "Sorry I stuck my licorice stick in your robot's neck without asking," said Jo.

As they began working on inventions, Melia didn't mind if Jo
rearranged things, or turned them upside down, or gave them
funny names. She realized that was Jo's way of working.

Melia helped with Jo's creations too. She concocted a gooey material they could use to make set pieces for Jo's dances. And homemade musical instruments they could play when Jo was singing her songs!

By combining Jo's art skills with Melia's science skills, they could create more super-cool stuff together than either could create alone.

When the robot waddled by, Melia said, "Let's call him Reynaldo the Licorice Neck Robot."

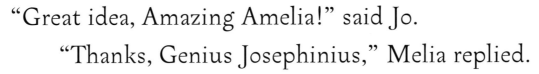

"Great idea, Amazing Amelia!" said Jo.

"Thanks, Genius Josephinius," Melia replied.

Reynaldo's licorice neck wouldn't last long. But the friendship between Melia and Jo would last forever.

aiRPlane

Melia made a plane that goes fast and far, with help from her cool friend Jo. You can make a plane that goes fast and far too, with help from a cool parent. Or a cool caregiver.

StaBilizeR

PRopelleR

Body

wings

tail

StRaw engine

MateRials

1 piece of paper
1 piece of card stock or index card
1 bendy straw
1 pencil slightly thicker than the straw
1 glue stick
1 push pin
1 pair of scissors

1 CUT SHAPES OUT OF PAPER

- For the body, cut out a rectangle.
- For the wings, cut out an oval.
- For the tail, cut out an oval.
- For the stabilizer, cut out half an oval.

2 DECORATE

- Decorate your plane with crayons, colored pencils, or markers.

3 CREATE THE BODY

- Roll the paper rectangle around the pencil to create a tube.
- Glue the tube along its side to seal it.
- Fold one end of the tube down and seal it with glue.
- Blow into the tube to make sure no air escapes from the sealed end.
- Take the pencil out after rolling and gluing the paper.

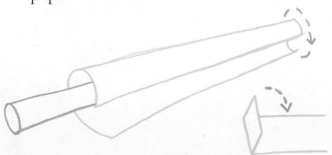

4 ATTACH WINGS, TAIL, AND STABILIZER

- Glue the wings and tail to the body.
- Fold a small flap on the stabilizer to create a stand.
- Apply glue to the stand and attach it to the top of the body.

5 CREATE THE PROPELLER

- Cut card stock into a propeller shape.
- Decorate the propeller.
- Attach the propeller to the front of the plane with a push pin.

6 FLY!

- Push the back of the plane onto the straw.
- Blow into the straw and watch your plane soar!

STEAM DREAM TEAM

Melia has strong STEM skills—she's really good at science, technology, engineering, and math. Jo's all about the arts—singing, dancing, painting, acting, and designing things. When you put an A for *arts* in STEM, you get STEAM.

Melia and Jo are a perfect STEAM team! They put their skills together to solve problems and make amazing creations.

How often do you use your STEAM skills? When using them, which of these words describe you?

Creative

Curious

Imaginative

Brave

Patient

Focused

Flexible

Daring

Observant

Persistent

Use your STEAM skills well, and they will power you ahead to cool solutions and amazing creations of your own!

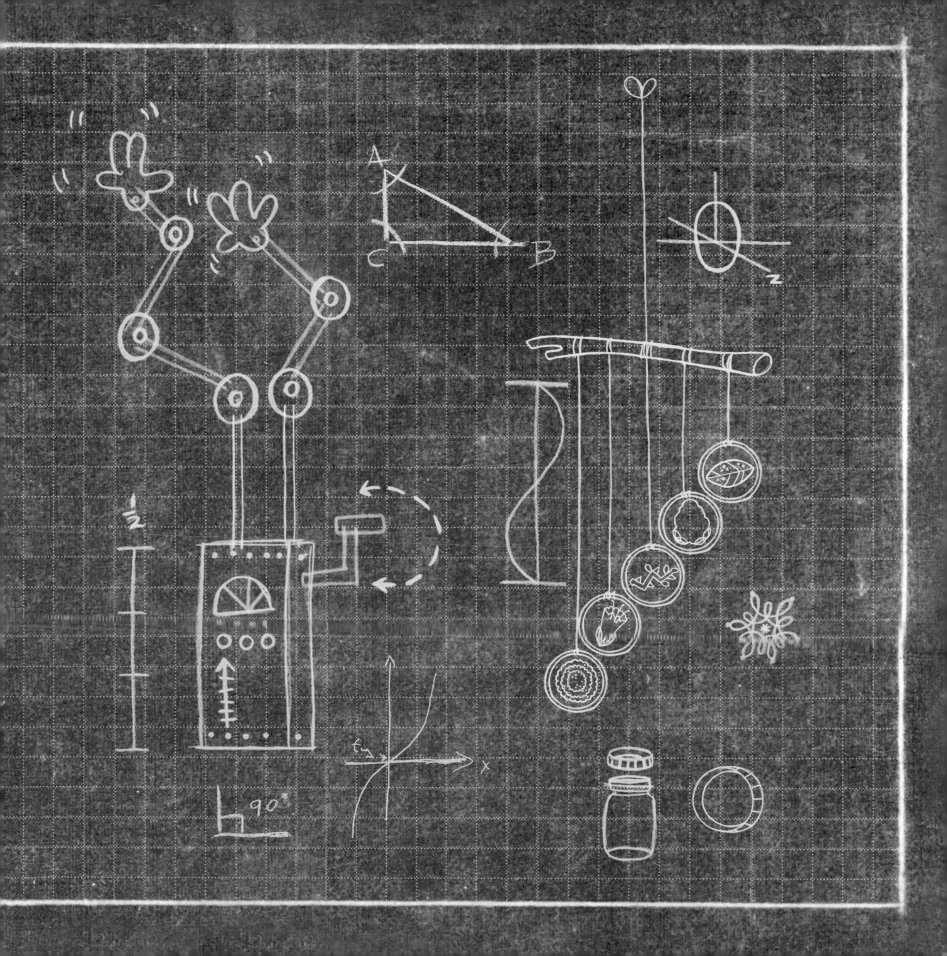